Toot and Puddle

by

Holly Hobbie

MACDONALD YOUNG BOOKS

Copyright © 1997 Holly Hobbie

First published in the US in 1997 by
Little, Brown & Company

First published in Britain in 1999 by
Macdonald Young Books
an imprint of Wayland Publishers Ltd
61 Western Road
Hove
East Sussex
BN3 1JD

A catalogue record for this book
is available from the British Library

ISBN 0 7500 2827 0

Toot and Puddle lived together in Woodcock Pocket.

It was such a perfect place to be that Puddle never wanted to go anywhere else.

Toot, on the other hand, loved to take trips. He had been to lots of different places.

One day in January, Toot decided to set off on his biggest trip ever. He decided to see the world. "Do you want to come along?" he asked Puddle. "We could start with somewhere warm and exciting."

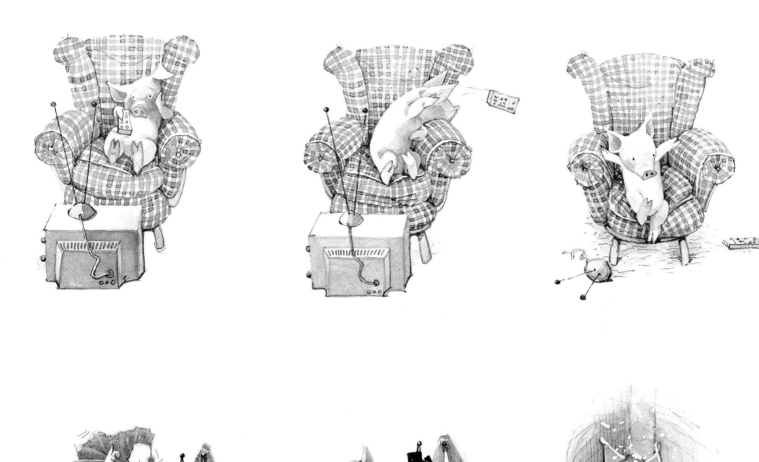

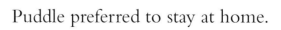

Puddle preferred to stay at home.

I love snow, he thought.

Meanwhile... presenting Puddle at Pocket Pond!

MARCH ON THE NILE

Dear Puddle,
Egypt is amazing.
The pyramids are
brilliant. Wish
you could meet
me at the oasis.
Your friend,
Toot

To: Puddle
Woodcock Pocket

PAR AVION

MARCH
NILE RIVER
PM

EGYPT

March meant maple syrup. Puddle wished Toot were there to taste the pancakes.

Dear Puddle,
Can you believe I'm
in the Solomon Islands?
They're in the Pacific
Ocean. I spend all day
underwater. I love
being in a school –
of fish! Has spring
come yet?
          Your pal,
          Toot

To: Puddle
Woodcock Pocket

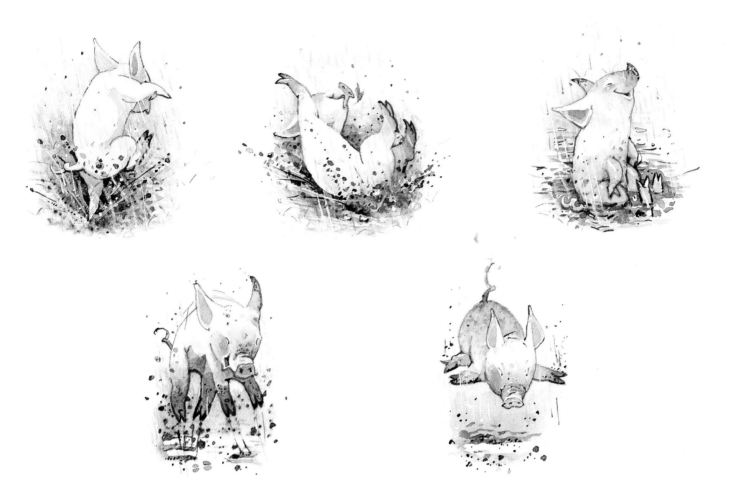

Yes, spring had arrived. Puddle was enjoying mud season. Yippee!

Back at Woodcock Pocket...
"For he's a jolly good fellow,
for he's a jolly good fellow,
for he's a jolly good fellow,
and so say all of us!"

Dear Puddle,
Help! Mountain
climbing is scarier
than jumping out of
a plane. Remember
when I talked you into
going parachuting?
Your friend in the Alps,
Toot

To: Puddle
Woodcock Pocket

Puddle remembered.

In July... presenting Puddle at Pocket Pond! Every time he jumped in, he cheered, *"Olé!"*

Dear Puddle,
August is cold in
Antarctica, but I've
made more friends
here than anywhere
yet. Are you going
to the beach this
year? I miss you.
Do you miss me?
Friends forever,
Toot

To: Puddle
Woodcock Pocket

Yes, Puddle missed his friend.

Dear Pudsy,
Bonjour from Paris!
Art is everywhere!
Love is in the air!

Au revoir,
Toot

To: Puddle
Woodcock Pocket

I love art, thought Puddle.

Dearest Pudsio,
Italy is heaven —
it's one big treat!
Your friend,
Tootsio

To: Puddle
Woodcock Pocket

VIA AEREA

OCTOBER
FLORENCE ITALY
AM

ITALY

Meanwhile, it was Hallowe'en in Woodcock Pocket.

Puddle decided to be horrifying.

One morning in November, Toot woke up and thought,
It's time to go home.

Yippee, Toot's coming!

December called for celebration.
"Here's to all your adventures around the world," said Puddle.
"Here's to all your adventures at home," said Toot.

"And here's to being together again," Toot and Puddle
said at the same time.

Toot was happy to be back in his own bed,
and Puddle was happy, too.

"I wonder if it will snow all night," Puddle said.
"I hope so," said Toot.
"Then we'll go sliding," said Puddle.
"And skiing," said Toot.
"Good night, Toot."
"Good night, Puddle."